The Long Sock

CATHERINE MALASKI • LISA PERRETT

Hi, Duck!

Hi, Chick!

Ding Dong!

That is a long sock!

I can put it on
my neck.

I can hang it on
my wing.

I can put a rock in it.

Duck, that is such a long sock.

That is my sock!

Chick	hang	rock
ding	long	sock
dong	neck	wing
Duck		

Decodable Words

can	it	such
in	on	

High-Frequency Words

a	is	put
hi	my	that
I		